Scary and Fun Stories for Fa[...]
Vampires Don't Drink Juice!

Disclaimer

📖 Read at Your Own Risk!

Ghoul-Free Guarantee: While this book dives into the spooky and supernatural, rest assured that no real ghosts, vampires, or other creepy creatures are included with your purchase. Any strange noises or mysterious shadows in your home are purely coincidental and not conjured by these pages.

Check Under the Bed: If these tales make you peek under the bed or hesitate before opening your closet, please note that the author is not responsible for any sleepless nights or newfound fears of the dark. Remember, it's all just part of the fun!

Reality Check: This book may transport you to eerie camps, haunted houses, and creepy forests, but you'll always find yourself safely back in your own room. No real vampires, rap battles with ghosts, or magical transformations will occur (no matter how much you practice your rhymes).

Attachment Warnings: If you find yourself unusually attached to the fates of any characters, living, undead, or spectral, understand that any emotional turmoil is part of the reading experience and completely your own to manage. Just try not to get too attached to those vampire puppies!

Vampire Disclaimer: No vampires, ancient or modern, were harmed in the making of these stories. Any resemblance to real vampires, living or undead, is purely coincidental. And no, vampires don't really engage in rap battles (at least, not that we know of).

All rights reserved © 2024

Contents

INTRODUCTION 5

The House on Vampire Hill 8
- CHAPTER 1: MOVING IN 9
- CHAPTER 2: STRANGE NOISES 13
- CHAPTER 3: THE MYSTERIOUS NEIGHBOR 17
- CHAPTER 4: DISCOVERING THE LAIR 20
- CHAPTER 5: THE PLAN 22
- CHAPTER 6: RESOLUTION 23

My Furry Little Vampire 26
- CHAPTER 1: THE DISCOVERY 27
- CHAPTER 2: STRANGE BEHAVIOR 30
- CHAPTER 3: THE REVEAL 33
- CHAPTER 4: THE BATTLE 36
- CHAPTER 5: AFTERMATH 39

The Vampire's Bloodthirsty Game 41
- CHAPTER 1: THE MYSTERIOUS YARD SALE 42
- CHAPTER 2: THE VAMPIRES ARRIVE 48
- CHAPTER 3: THE BATTLE OF WITS 53
- CHAPTER 4: THE FINAL SHOWDOWN 55
- CHAPTER 5: THE AFTERMATH 58

The Blood Red Lake 62
Chapter 1: The Discovery 63
Chapter 2: The Red Sunset 69
Chapter 3: The Vampire's Plea 73
Chapter 4: The Ritual 76
Chapter 5: The Greater Evil 81

Camp Bloodwood 88
Chapter 1: The Legend Begins 89
Chapter 2: Strange Happenings 93
Chapter 3: Unveiling Secrets 96
Chapter 4: The Truth Revealed 99
Chapter 5: A New Beginning 102

INTRODUCTION

Ready to sink your teeth into a world of spooky fun? Get ready to dive into a collection of five fang-tastic tales that will whisk you away to the eerie and mysterious realm of vampires. Each story is packed with suspense, courage, and plenty of laugh-out-loud moments, perfect for curious minds who love a good scare.

Grab your garlic, sharpen your wooden stakes, and get ready for a wild ride through dark hallways, spooky forests, and, yes, even a vampire puppy! Don't forget to pack your sense of humor—you'll need it when you're outsmarting vampires and wondering if your dog has suddenly developed a taste for raw steak!

The House on Vampire Hill

Imagine moving into a creepy old house that whispers secrets through its creaky floors and dark hallways. Strange noises in the night, hidden lairs, and a mysterious neighbor who knows more than he lets on—what would you do? Just don't forget to bring your garlic and wooden stakes! And remember, if you hear a creak, it's probably just the house... or is it?

My Furry Little Vampire

What if you found a cute, scruffy puppy with a big secret? This little pet has an unusual craving and an aversion to

sunlight. Can you solve the mystery and uncover the truth about your new furry friend? And what would you do if your dog started demanding raw steak for dinner? Maybe it's time to invest in a doggy sunscreen!

The Vampire's Bloodthirsty Game

Discover an old, spooky board game at a yard sale and unleash ancient vampires into your living room. The only way to survive is to play the game and win. Will you dare to roll the dice, solve the riddles, and outsmart the vampires? Just be sure to keep some garlic bread nearby, you never know when it might come in handy. And seriously, who knew board games could be this intense?

The Blood Red Lake

Stumble upon a hidden lake that turns blood-red at sunset and is said to be haunted by a cursed vampire. As you explore, you uncover secrets that lead to a dangerous ritual. Can you break the curse without unleashing a greater evil? And seriously, why does the water look like tomato soup? Maybe it's time to pack some extra breadsticks!

Camp Bloodwood

Welcome to the spookiest, most exciting camp experience of your life—Camp Bloodwood! Do you have the guts to investigate those creepy noises outside your cabin at night? What if your camp counselors are hiding supernatural secrets? And just when you think you've seen it all, prepare

for the most epic rap battle against the ghostly camp counselors! Can you out-rhyme a vampire with centuries of practice?

Are you brave enought to handle the chills and thrills, or will you be hiding under your blanket by the end? Let's find out—if you dare!

The House on Vampire Hill

Chapter 1: Moving In

The moving van rumbled up the steep, winding road to Vampire Hill, a name that had sent shivers down Ben's spine ever since his dad announced the move. Ben leaned out the window, squinting at the towering house that loomed ahead. It looked like something from a horror movie, with its dark, weathered wood and broken shutters. He gulped.

"This place looks like it's straight out of a horror movie," Ben muttered.

His younger sister, Lily, peered out from the other window. "You mean, a vampire movie. I heard the hill is infamous for vampire sightings."

Their dad chuckled from the front seat. "Relax, it's just an old house. No vampires here, unless they're paying rent!"

Ben tried to laugh, but the house, with its creaky floors and dusty windows, seemed to laugh back at him. The old trees around the house cast long, twisted shadows, making it look even more foreboding.

As they got out of the car, their mom glanced at the house and frowned. "Well, it's definitely got character."

"Character is one word for it," Ben mumbled under his breath.

"Come on, you two," their dad said, trying to sound upbeat. "Let's get inside and start unpacking."

They trudged up the creaky steps to the front door. As their dad turned the key in the lock, it gave way with a loud, eerie creak. The door swung open, revealing a dark, musty foyer.

"Home sweet home," their dad declared, stepping inside. His voice echoed through the empty halls.

Ben and Lily exchanged uneasy glances. They followed their parents inside, each step on the old wooden floorboards echoing through the empty rooms. The air inside was cool and smelled faintly of mildew.

As they explored the house, they found more and more signs of its age. The wallpaper was peeling in places, revealing ancient plaster underneath. The light fixtures were old-fashioned, and some didn't work at all. The furniture, left by the previous owners, was covered in sheets and layers of dust.

"Okay, everyone, start unloading the van," their mom instructed. "We've got a lot of work to do."

Ben and Lily shared a resigned sigh and headed back outside to help. They lugged boxes and furniture up the steps and into the house, each item a reminder of how much work lay ahead.

Once the van was unloaded, their mom called them into the kitchen. "How about some lunch before we start unpacking?"

They sat around the old wooden table, eating sandwiches and sipping lemonade. The mood was somber, the excitement of the move dampened by the eerie atmosphere of their new home.

After lunch, Ben and Lily decided to take a break from unpacking and explore the house. They wandered into a dimly lit hallway, lined with ancient portraits of stern-looking ancestors. The eyes in the paintings seemed to follow them as they walked by.

Lily nudged Ben and pointed to the attic door. "Check out this huge attic! Perfect for storing coffins."

Ben rolled his eyes. "Or maybe it's where they keep the bats."

Lily laughed. "Bat joke? That's so last century, Ben."

They climbed up to the attic and found it filled with old, dusty furniture and cobwebs. In the corner, a large,

faded painting caught their eye. It depicted a sinister-looking man with sharp teeth, glaring at them as if he knew their deepest fears.

"This is officially the creepiest attic ever," Ben said, shivering despite himself.

"You're telling me," Lily replied, inching closer to Ben.

The attic was filled with old trunks and covered furniture. Dust motes danced in the light filtering through a small, grimy window. As they explored further, they found a small, ornate chest tucked away in a corner.

"Look at this!" Lily exclaimed, brushing off the dust. She lifted the lid, revealing a collection of old letters and photographs.

Ben picked up a yellowed letter and squinted at the faded writing. "It's in some weird language. Probably ancient vampire script."

Lily giggled. "Or maybe it's just really bad handwriting."

They continued to sift through the chest's contents, finding old jewelry, a broken pocket watch, and more letters. Each item seemed to tell a story, adding to the mysterious aura of the attic.

Suddenly, the floorboards creaked loudly behind them. They spun around, hearts pounding, but saw nothing but shadows.

"Okay, that's enough exploring for today," Ben said, his voice shaking slightly. "Let's go help Mom and Dad."

Lily nodded, and they hurried back down the stairs, leaving the chest and its secrets behind.

Chapter 2: Strange Noises

As Ben and Lily settled into their new rooms that night, strange sounds filled the air. Ben tossed and turned in his bed, unable to shake the feeling that someone, or something, was watching him. Just as he was about to drift off, a scratching sound made him bolt upright.

"Do you hear that? It's coming from the walls," Ben whispered to Lily, who was lying in the next bed, wide-eyed.

"Maybe it's a vampire sharpening its claws," Lily suggested, her voice trembling slightly.

"Or a very ambitious mouse," Ben joked, trying to lighten the mood.

The scratching grew louder and more frantic, as if whatever was making the noise was desperate to get out.

The siblings lay still, too scared to move, until the noise finally subsided just before dawn.

Ben stared at the ceiling, wide awake, his mind racing. He couldn't shake the image of something with long, sharp claws trapped inside the walls, trying to break free.

As the first light of dawn filtered through the curtains, he finally drifted off to sleep, exhausted and unnerved.

The next day, Ben and Lily woke up feeling groggy and unsettled. They ate breakfast in silence, the memory of the night's events still fresh in their minds. Their parents, oblivious to their children's distress, chatted cheerfully about their plans for the day.

"We've got a lot of unpacking to do," their mom said, sipping her coffee. "And I want to start cleaning out the basement."

Ben and Lily exchanged a worried glance. The basement sounded like the last place they wanted to be, especially after hearing those noises.

After breakfast, Ben and Lily decided to investigate the source of the noise. They armed themselves with flashlights and ventured into the hallway.

"We need to find out what's making that noise," Ben said, his voice resolute.

Lily nodded. "Agreed, but we better bring a flashlight and some garlic."

"Don't forget the wooden stakes. You know, just in case," Ben added with a grin.

They followed the sound to a small door under the staircase. It creaked open to reveal a dark, cramped crawl space. Ben shone his flashlight inside, and they both gasped. The walls were covered in strange claw marks, deep and jagged, as if something with long, sharp nails had been trapped there.

"This is seriously creepy," Lily whispered. "What could have made these?"

"I don't know," Ben replied, "but I have a feeling we're going to find out."

They crawled further into the space, their flashlights casting eerie shadows on the walls. The air was cold and damp, and the smell of mildew was overpowering.

At the far end of the crawl space, they found a small, wooden door, barely visible in the dim light.

"Do you think this is where the noise is coming from?" Lily asked, her voice barely above a whisper.

"Only one way to find out," Ben replied, reaching for the handle.

The door creaked open, revealing a narrow, twisting staircase leading down into the darkness.

"Great, another creepy staircase," Lily muttered.

They descended the stairs cautiously, each step echoing in the narrow space. The further down they went, the colder it got, until their breath was visible in the dim light.

At the bottom of the stairs, they found themselves in a small, stone chamber. The walls were lined with more claw marks, and the air was thick with the smell of damp earth.

"This place is giving me the creeps," Ben said, shining his flashlight around the room.

"Me too," Lily agreed. "Let's get out of here."

They hurried back up the stairs and out of the crawl space, relieved to be back in the relative safety of the hallway.

CHAPTER 3: THE MYSTERIOUS NEIGHBOR

Later that day, as Ben and Lily played outside, a shadow fell over them. They looked up to see a tall, gaunt man with piercing eyes standing at the edge of their yard. He wore an old-fashioned suit and a wide-brimmed hat that cast a sinister shadow over his face.

"Welcome to Vampire Hill," he said in a low, gravelly voice. "You should be careful at night."

Ben felt a chill run down his spine. "Why? Because of vampires?"

The man smirked. "Perhaps."

Always quick with a comeback, Lily tilted her head and asked, "Do you get a discount for being spooky, or does it come naturally?"

The man's smirk widened. "A little of both, I suppose. I'm Mr. Thorn, your neighbor."

"Mr. Thorn, do you know anything about the strange noises in our house?" Ben asked, trying to sound casual.

Mr. Thorn's eyes seemed to glint in the fading daylight. "Strange noises, you say? This house does have a history."

"What kind of history?" Lily pressed, her curiosity piqued.

Mr. Thorn leaned in closer, lowering his voice. "Let's just say it's been home to many... unusual residents. Some say the house itself is alive."

Ben and Lily exchanged uneasy glances. Mr. Thorn's cryptic words only deepened their sense of dread.

As Mr. Thorn handed them an old key with strange symbols etched into it, he spoke in riddles.

"The house has secrets. Some doors are better left closed," he warned.

Lily frowned. "Is that a riddle or a threat?"

Ben tried to lighten the mood. "Sounds like he moonlights as a fortune cookie writer."

Mr. Thorn's expression didn't change. "Just a friendly warning. Be careful."

With that, he turned and walked away, leaving Ben and Lily more curious—and frightened—than ever.

"Do you think he's serious?" Lily asked, turning the key over in her hands.

"I don't know," Ben replied, "but we should probably be careful. Just in case."

They watched Mr. Thorn disappear into the shadows, the key feeling heavy in Lily's hand. As they headed back inside, they couldn't shake the feeling that they were being watched.

As they sat down to dinner that evening, their dad mentioned meeting Mr. Thorn.

"Seems like a nice enough guy," he said. "A bit odd, but friendly."

Ben and Lily exchanged a glance, deciding not to mention the key or Mr. Thorn's warnings. They didn't want to worry their parents any more than they already were.

After dinner, they retreated to their rooms, the weight of the day's events pressing down on them. They lay in their beds, staring at the ceiling, trying to make sense of everything.

"Ben, do you think there really could be vampires?" Lily asked in a whisper.

"I don't know, Lil," Ben replied. "But whatever it is, we'll figure it out. Together."

Lily nodded, feeling a bit more reassured. With that, they finally drifted off to sleep, the key tucked safely under Lily's pillow.

CHAPTER 4: DISCOVERING THE LAIR

The next morning, determined to uncover the house's secrets, Ben and Lily took the strange key and began searching for a matching lock. Their search led them to the basement, a dark and musty place filled with old boxes and cobwebs.

"This key must fit somewhere. Let's try the basement," Ben suggested.

Lily hesitated. "Just our luck — another creepy place to explore."

"At least it's not the attic again. That place gives me the heebie-jeebies," Ben replied.

In the far corner of the basement, they found a small, inconspicuous door. The key fit perfectly. With a creak, the door opened to reveal a dark staircase leading underground.

"Do we really have to go down there?" Lily asked, her voice shaking slightly.

"We have to find out what's going on," Ben replied, trying to sound braver than he felt.

They descended the stairs cautiously, each step echoing in the narrow space. The further down they went, the colder it got, until their breath was visible in the dim light.

At the bottom of the stairs, they found themselves in a cavernous room filled with ancient relics and, to their horror, coffins.

"I knew it! Vampires!" Ben exclaimed, his voice echoing in the dark.

"We have to get out of here before they wake up!" Lily whispered urgently.

"Do you think they have vampire alarm clocks?" Ben joked, trying to mask his fear.

As they backed away, shadows seemed to move on their own, and a cold, eerie breeze swept through the room.

"We need to go, now," Ben insisted.

They turned to leave, but the sound of a coffin lid creaking open froze them in their tracks.

"Did you hear that?" Lily whispered, clutching Ben's arm.

"Yeah, and I don't think it's good news," Ben replied, backing away slowly.

The lid of one of the coffins slid open, and a pale hand with long, sharp nails emerged, followed by the rest of a gaunt, menacing figure.

"Run!" Ben shouted, grabbing Lily's hand and pulling her towards the stairs.

They scrambled up the stairs, their hearts pounding, and slammed the door shut behind them.

CHAPTER 5: THE PLAN

Back in the basement, they quickly sealed the hidden door and leaned against it, catching their breath.

"What do we do now?" Lily asked, her voice shaking.

"We need a plan," Ben replied, thinking quickly. "We have to find a way to keep them trapped down there."

As they tried to escape, they found their path blocked by the vampires, who had awakened and now surrounded them, their eyes glowing red in the darkness.

"You should have stayed out of our lair," the vampire leader hissed.

"Run, Lily!" Ben shouted, pushing her towards the stairs.

Lily, ever defiant, glared at the vampires. "Do I look like a vampire snack to you?"

Thinking quickly, Lily spotted an old mirror propped against the wall. She grabbed it and held it up, reflecting the vampires' faces back at them.

"Over here! Use the old mirror!" Lily yelled.

Ben caught on and helped her position the mirror. The vampires hissed and recoiled, their glowing eyes dimming as they were confronted with their own reflections.

"Good thinking! Vampires hate their reflection!" Ben exclaimed.

"Curse you and your reflective surfaces!" one of the vampires snarled, retreating further into the shadows.

With the vampires temporarily thwarted, Ben and Lily managed to scramble up the stairs and slam the door shut behind them.

CHAPTER 6: RESOLUTION

Back in the basement, they quickly sealed the hidden door and hid the key, hoping to keep the vampires trapped for good.

"This should keep them trapped for a while," Ben said, panting.

"And we'll make sure no one else finds that key," Lily added, slipping it into her pocket.

"Maybe we should mail it to Mr. Thorn as a thank you gift," Ben joked.

As they secured the door, the house seemed to sigh in relief, the oppressive atmosphere lifting slightly.

"We did it," Lily said, leaning against the wall. "We really did it."

Ben nodded, feeling a sense of accomplishment wash over him. "Yeah, we did. But we have to stay vigilant. Just in case."

The next day, the family continued to settle in, unaware of the harrowing adventure Ben and Lily had experienced.

"You kids have quite the imagination!" their dad remarked, noticing their tired expressions.

"Yeah, just a wild adventure," Ben replied, exchanging a knowing look with Lily.
"Next time, let's move to a place with fewer vampires," Lily suggested, smiling.
As they settled into their new routine, a faint scratching sound echoed through the walls, a reminder that their

adventure might not be over just yet. The siblings shared a glance, knowing that they had to stay vigilant. The house on Vampire Hill had secrets, and some doors were better left closed.

My Furry Little Vampire

Chapter 1: The Discovery

Max, an 11-year-old with a knack for curiosity, was heading home from school, kicking a pebble along the sidewalk. The sky was a mix of orange and pink hues as the sun began to set. Suddenly, he heard a faint whimpering sound coming from a nearby alley. Intrigued, he followed the sound and found a small, scruffy puppy sitting alone, shivering behind a garbage can.

Max knelt down and extended a hand. "Oh, look at you! Who left you all alone, buddy?" he said softly.

The puppy's eyes glistened as it gazed up at Max. Though it couldn't speak, it thought to itself, "You have no idea what you're in for, kid."

Max grinned and decided then and there that he couldn't leave the puppy behind. "I'll call you Fang. Those tiny teeth are hilarious!" he chuckled, noticing the puppy's small, sharp fangs peeking out from its mouth.

Fang wagged his tail enthusiastically. "Sure, laugh now, kid. Wait till you see me at midnight," he thought, rolling his eyes internally.

Max glanced around, making sure no one else was watching, then scooped the puppy into his arms. Fang

snuggled against him, feeling surprisingly warm despite his shivering. As Max walked, he could feel Fang's heartbeat racing, mirroring his own excitement and nervousness.

With Fang nestled in his arms, Max hurried home, hoping his parents would let him keep the puppy.

Max tiptoed into the house, careful not to alert his parents. He snuck Fang up to his room and set him on the bed. The puppy immediately started sniffing around, inspecting its new surroundings. Fang seemed especially interested in the shadows cast by Max's bedside lamp, pouncing on them as if they were alive.

Max closed the door and whispered, "Mom, can I keep him? I promise he won't eat much... hopefully."

Fang, curling up on Max's pillow, thought, "Famous last words, kid. Famous last words."

A knock on the door made Max jump. His mom, Mrs. Thompson, peeked in. "Max, what are you up to in there?"

Max took a deep breath. "Mom, I found this puppy. Can we keep him? I'll take good care of him, I swear."

Mrs. Thompson looked at Fang, who gave her the most innocent puppy eyes. She sighed, "As long as you're responsible, Max. And remember, no biting!"

Max beamed. "Thanks, Mom! I promise he'll be the best-behaved puppy ever!"

Fang thought, "Yeah, the best-behaved vampire puppy ever. Good luck, Max."

That evening, Max tried to feed Fang some dog food. He placed the bowl on the floor and waited for Fang to eat.

"Here you go, Fang. Yummy dog food!" Max said, patting the puppy's head.

Fang sniffed the food and wrinkled his nose. "Sniff...sniff... Is this a joke? Where's the steak?" Fang thought, clearly unimpressed.

Max frowned. "You don't like it? Weird. Maybe you're just not hungry."

As night fell, Max settled into bed, but he was awoken by strange noises coming from the kitchen. He tiptoed downstairs to find Fang gnawing on a raw steak. Fang looked up, eyes wide, meat hanging from his mouth.

Max's eyes widened. "Mom's gonna flip when she sees the steak missing. Let's keep this between us, okay, Fang?"

Fang glanced at Max, raw steak in his mouth, and thought, "Deal, kid. For now."

Max crept back to his room, shaking his head in disbelief. "A puppy with a taste for raw steak? This is going to be interesting."

Fang, licking his lips, settled back on Max's pillow, thinking, "You have no idea, Max. No idea at all."

Chapter 2: Strange Behavior

Over the next few days, Max noticed Fang's unusual eating habits. Raw meat disappeared from the fridge regularly, and Max's attempts to feed Fang dog food always ended in failure. Fang would turn his nose up at the kibble and look at Max as if saying, "Is this a joke?"

Max scratched his head. "Why do you only eat raw meat, Fang? Are you on some kind of paleo diet?"

Fang, chewing on a piece of raw chicken, thought, "More like a Transylvanian diet."

Max's parents began to notice the missing meat. One evening, Mrs. Thompson opened the fridge and gasped. "Max, why is there a steak in your room? Were you planning a midnight barbecue?"

Max stammered, "Uh, no, Mom. Must have been a mistake. I'll put it back."

Fang rolled his eyes. "Smooth, Max. Real smooth," he thought, hiding a chicken wing under the bed.

Mr. Thompson also began to notice the food shortages. "Max, is there something you're not telling us about where all the raw meat is going?" he asked one night during dinner.

Max, trying to avoid suspicion, quickly said, "Maybe the fridge is haunted by a meat-loving ghost."

Fang, hiding under the table, thought, "Close enough."

Max soon realized that Fang was much more active at night. He often heard the puppy padding around the house in the dark, only to find Fang back in his bed by morning.

"Fang, where do you keep disappearing to? Got a secret doggy disco?" Max asked one night.

Fang, lying on his back with his paws in the air, thought, "If only you knew, Max. If only you knew."

One evening, Max noticed Fang's eyes glowing in the dark. "Whoa, your eyes glow in the dark! Cool, but also kinda creepy," Max said, watching Fang's eerie gaze.

Fang just blinked slowly. "Nothing to see here, just your average, everyday vampire puppy."

Max shook his head and decided he needed to figure out what was going on. He started keeping a notebook of Fang's activities, jotting down every strange thing Fang did. The list grew longer every day, filled with notes about missing meat, glowing eyes, and nocturnal adventures.

Concerned about Fang's strange behavior, Max decided to do some research. He spent hours on the internet, looking up everything he could about glowing eyes and raw meat cravings.

"Let's see... glowing eyes, raw meat... Are you a dog or a Dracula wannabe?" Max muttered to himself.

Curled up on the bed, Fang thought, "A little of column A, a little of column B."

Max's worry grew. "This is nuts. I'm Googling 'vampire puppies' and getting actual results!" he exclaimed, staring at his computer screen in disbelief.

Fang peeked at the screen and thought, "Uh-oh. This kid's onto something."

Max stumbled upon a forum dedicated to vampire pets. He read stories from people claiming their pets had

similar behaviors. One user, "VampireVet101," described a list of symptoms that matched Fang perfectly: aversion to sunlight, preference for raw meat, and nocturnal activity.

Max sat back in his chair, rubbing his temples. "This can't be real. But what if it is?"

Fang stretched out, yawning, and thought, "Keep connecting the dots, kid. You're almost there."

Max also found an old book in the school library about local legends, including one about a vampire dog that had supposedly haunted the town centuries ago. The legend mentioned a dog with glowing eyes that only ate raw meat and was active only at night. Max couldn't believe how closely the description matched Fang.

"Fang, are you some kind of ancient vampire dog?" Max wondered aloud.

Fang, lounging on Max's bed, thought, "Bingo."

Chapter 3: The Reveal

One evening, Max was almost caught by his parents with Fang in his room. He heard footsteps approaching and quickly whispered, "Quick, Fang, hide! Mom's coming!"

Fang dashed under the bed, thinking, "Time for my best 'innocent puppy' face. Nailed it."

Mrs. Thompson entered the room, looking around suspiciously. "Why is there a blanket moving? Max, are you hiding snacks again?"

Max chuckled nervously. "No, Mom. Just tidying up."

Mrs. Thompson gave him a long look but eventually shrugged and left. Max let out a sigh of relief as Fang emerged from his hiding spot.

Fang shook his head and thought, "These close calls are getting old."

Late one night, Max woke up to find Fang standing on his chest, his eyes glowing brighter than ever.

"Fang, what are you doing on my chest? Are you trying to give me doggy CPR?" Max joked, half-asleep.

To his shock, Fang began to grow larger, his features becoming more menacing. "Actually, I'm planning something much more... eternal," Fang said, his voice low and eerie.

Max's eyes widened. "Okay, now you're talking! Wait, talking? You're a talking vampire dog!"

Fang grinned, his fangs gleaming. "Surprise, Max! Welcome to the night life."

Max bolted upright, nearly throwing Fang off the bed. "This is insane! What are you?"

Fang sat calmly, licking a paw. "I thought you'd never ask. I'm a vampire, Max. A vampire puppy, to be exact."

Max's mind raced. "But... how? Why?"

Fang sighed. "Long story. But right now, we've got bigger problems. Your garlic necklace is a bit too close for comfort."

Max grabbed the garlic necklace from his dresser and held it up. "Garlic necklace, holy water...I feel like I'm prepping for a Halloween party," Max muttered.

Fang hissed and retreated, clearly affected by the garlic. "Sorry, Max, but this is the end of our little friendship."

Max steeled himself. "Not if I have anything to say about it. Take that, Fang!"

Max waved the garlic necklace at Fang, who whimpered and backed away further.

"You're not getting away that easy," Max said, his voice shaking but determined.

Fang looked genuinely hurt. "C'mon, Max. We were buddies."

Max shook his head. "Buddies don't sneak around and steal steaks at night. Or, you know, turn out to be vampire dogs!"

Fang sighed dramatically. "Okay, okay. You got me. But I didn't choose this life, Max. It chose me."

Max paused. "What do you mean?"

Fang looked down. "I was bitten by a vampire bat when I was just a pup. Next thing I knew, I had this insatiable craving for raw meat and a serious aversion to sunlight."

Max frowned. "That's... actually kind of sad."

Fang nodded. "Tell me about it. Now, can we please figure out a way to fix this?"

CHAPTER 4: THE BATTLE

Max confided in his best friend, Grace, who was initially skeptical.

"Grace, you won't believe this, but Fang's a vampire!" Max said urgently.

Grace rolled her eyes. "Yeah, and I'm the Tooth Fairy. Wait, you're serious?"

Max nodded. "Serious as a steak shortage, Grace. We need to stock up on garlic."

Grace's eyes widened. "Okay, now you're scaring me. But if it's true, let's do this!"

The duo gathered supplies: garlic, holy water, and a mirror. They returned to Max's house, ready to confront Fang.

Max and Grace sneaked into Max's room, where Fang was waiting. The air felt electric with tension.

"Okay, Fang, time to face the garlic!" Max declared, holding up a clove.

Fang scoffed. "You kids and your silly garlic. It's more of an annoyance than a deterrent."

Max grinned. "Maybe, but annoying you is our specialty!"

Grace added, "Yeah, we're experts at that."

They surrounded Fang, who looked more amused than frightened. "You really think you can beat me with garlic and holy water?" Fang said, baring his fangs.

A tense battle ensued. Max and Grace used their supplies to weaken Fang, who grew weaker with each attack. The

atmosphere was eerie, with shadows dancing on the walls and Fang's eyes glowing menacingly.

"Fang, this is for all the missing steaks!" Max shouted, throwing holy water at the puppy.

Fang snarled, dodging the water. "You can't defeat me that easily, Max!"

Grace threw a garlic clove, hitting Fang on the nose. "Gotcha!"

Fang hissed, his eyes glowing brighter. "Enough! I'm done playing games."

Max held up the mirror, reflecting Fang's glowing eyes. "Look into your own eyes, Fang!"

Fang stared at his reflection, momentarily distracted. Max quickly tied the garlic necklace around Fang's neck.

Fang whimpered and started shrinking. His fangs retracted, and his eyes returned to normal. He fell to the floor, exhausted.

Max and Grace watched in awe. "Did we just turn him back into a regular puppy?" Max asked.

Grace nodded. "Looks like it. I guess garlic really is a vampire's worst nightmare."

Fang, now a normal puppy again, looked up at Max and Grace with wide, innocent eyes. He wagged his tail and barked softly.

Max reached down and picked up Fang, cradling him in his arms. "I guess we're back to square one, huh, buddy?"

Grace grinned. "Just make sure to keep the garlic handy. You never know when he might get a craving for raw meat again."

CHAPTER 5: AFTERMATH

Max and Grace cleaned up the basement, disposed of the raw meat, and made sure no traces of Fang's nocturnal activities remained.

"So, what do we do with this garlic necklace now?" Grace asked.

Max shook his head. "I think I'll keep it. Mom will never know."

Max's parents were none the wiser, believing the puppy had simply settled down.

Grace smirked. "Just make sure not to tell her where her steaks went."

Life slowly returned to normal for Max, though he remained cautious around stray animals.

"Hey, Grace, look at this garlic necklace. Think I should wear it as a fashion statement?" Max joked.

Grace laughed. "If you want to repel both vampires and people, sure."

Max grinned. "Better safe than sorry, right?"

He kept the garlic necklace as a reminder of his encounter with Fang.

One day, Max found a mysterious note in his locker, warning him that Fang was just one of many vampire creatures.

"A note? 'More vampires will come for you.' Great, just what I needed," Max sighed.

Grace looked over his shoulder. "Looks like our adventures are just beginning, Max."

Max smiled, a mix of excitement and caution in his eyes. "Well, at least we're prepared. Who knew garlic could be so useful?"

And so, Max's adventure with the supernatural was far from over, but with his best friend by his side and a garlic necklace around his neck, he felt ready for whatever came next.

The Vampire's Bloodthirsty Game

Chapter 1: The Mysterious Yard Sale

Mia loved Saturdays. Not because it meant no school, but because of the yard sales. There was something magical about sifting through other people's old stuff, finding hidden treasures that were just waiting to be discovered. This Saturday morning was no different. The sun was shining, birds were chirping, and the streets of her neighborhood were lined with tables covered in trinkets and treasures.

Mia, a 12-year-old girl with a passion for adventure and mystery, had a keen eye for finding the unusual. She was always on the lookout for something that could spark a new adventure. Her best friend Alex, who shared her love for all things mysterious, was by her side as usual. Alex was always ready with a joke or a funny comment, which made their explorations even more enjoyable.

Mia was the youngest in her family, with two older brothers who constantly challenged her to think on her feet. This made her quick-witted and determined, traits that would soon prove invaluable. Alex, the class clown, was always ready to make Mia laugh but was fiercely loyal to his friends. His dad was a police officer, which inspired Alex's bravery and quick thinking.

"Alright, Mia, what are we hunting for today?" Alex asked, juggling a soccer ball with his knees.

Mia grinned. "Anything that looks old and spooky. The creepier, the better!"

They walked down the street, stopping at each yard sale, digging through boxes of old books, toys, and knick-knacks. It wasn't until they reached Mrs. Jenkins' yard sale that they found something truly intriguing.

Mrs. Jenkins' yard sale was known for its vast array of oddities. Mrs. Jenkins herself was a bit of an enigma—an older woman with thick glasses and a penchant for the peculiar. Today, her tables were filled with everything from antique lamps to old board games.

"Look at this, Alex," Mia said, pulling out an old, dusty box from under a pile of books. The box was labeled "The Vampire's Bloodthirsty Game."

Alex peeked over her shoulder. "Cool! Does it come with garlic bread?"

Mia laughed. "I think it's more of a 'play if you dare' kind of thing, not 'play if you're hungry.'"

Mrs. Jenkins noticed their interest and shuffled over. "Oh, that old thing? It's been in my attic for years. Came

with the house when I bought it. You can have it for a dollar."

Mia handed over a crumpled bill without hesitation. As they walked away, Mrs. Jenkins called after them, "Be careful with that, kids. It's been known to cause a bit of a... bite."

"Awesome, a board game with bite-sized fun! Or should I say, fun-sized bites?" Alex joked, grinning widely.

Mia shook her head, smiling. "Come on, let's go check it out."

Back at Mia's house, they rushed to her room with the game. The box was old and worn, the artwork detailed and spooky, featuring a dark castle under a blood-red moon, surrounded by bats and shadowy figures. It was perfect.

"This is going to be so much fun," Mia said, opening the box. Inside, they found a game board, a set of rules written in old-fashioned script, tiny coffins, vampire hunters, and a mysterious blood-red die.

Alex picked up the rules and squinted at them. "Why does it say, 'Do not play after midnight'? Are the vampires allergic to late-night snacks?"

Mia shrugged. "Maybe they turn into cranky bats if they don't get their beauty sleep."

"Or maybe they're just afraid of my breath after I eat garlic pizza," Alex added, making Mia laugh.

They spread the game out on the floor, reading the cryptic instructions. The game seemed straightforward enough: move around the board, complete challenges, and avoid the vampires.

"This is going to be awesome," Alex said, picking up one of the tiny vampire hunter pieces. "Let's do this!"

And so, with a mixture of excitement and a hint of nervousness, they began their adventure, completely unaware of the real danger that awaited them.

Mia and Alex could hardly contain their excitement as they set up the game in Mia's living room. The instructions were old and a bit hard to read, but they managed to piece together how to set up the board and the game pieces.

"Look at these tiny coffins," Mia said, setting them up in a neat row. "And the vampire hunters look so serious."

"Serious? They look like they're on a mission to find the nearest bathroom," Alex quipped, making Mia giggle.

The board itself was a detailed map of a dark, gothic landscape, complete with haunted castles, shadowy forests, and eerie graveyards. Each space had its own unique challenge or trap, making it clear that this game was designed to be as thrilling as it was spooky.

"Why does it feel like we're about to step into a horror movie?" Alex asked, his voice tinged with excitement.

"Because we kind of are," Mia replied. "Now, who's going first?"

They decided to let fate choose, rolling the blood-red die to see who would make the first move. Alex won, and with a dramatic flourish, he moved his vampire hunter piece onto the first space.

As Alex's piece landed on the first space, the room seemed to grow colder. Mia shivered, but chalked it up to excitement.

"Alright, Alex, what does your first space say?" she asked.

Alex read the space aloud, "Beware the shadows, for they hold secrets untold. Answer this riddle, and your journey will unfold."

Mia raised an eyebrow. "A riddle? Easy peasy. What's the riddle?"

Alex flipped over a card and read it, "I have cities, but no houses. I have mountains, but no trees. I have water, but no fish. What am I?"

Mia thought for a moment before answering, "A map!"

The room seemed to grow warmer again, and Alex's piece moved forward on its own. "Nice job, Mia! Now it's your turn."

Mia rolled the die and landed on a space that said, "Release the Vampire."

"Uh, Alex, I think this space is broken," Mia said nervously.

Suddenly, the lights flickered, and a cold draft swept through the room. Mia and Alex looked at each other, their earlier humor replaced with genuine unease.

"Did you feel that cold draft? It's like a ghost just walked through," Mia said, her voice shaky.

"Or maybe Dad just left the fridge open again," Alex joked, trying to lighten the mood.

But before Mia could respond, a dark, swirling mist began to form in the center of the room. They watched in horror as the mist coalesced into the shape of a tall, menacing figure with pale skin, sharp fangs, and glowing red eyes. His black cloak billowed as if caught in

a supernatural wind, and his eyes locked onto them with a hunger that chilled them to the bone.

"Who dares to release Count Vlad from his slumber?" the figure bellowed.

Mia and Alex stood frozen, unable to believe their eyes. The vampire was real, and he was standing right in front of them.

"Great. I hope he's not a morning person," Alex muttered, his earlier bravado fading fast.

As the vampire advanced towards them, they realized that this was no ordinary board game. They had unleashed something ancient and dangerous, and their only hope of survival was to play the game and win.

CHAPTER 2: THE VAMPIRES ARRIVE

Count Vlad loomed over Mia and Alex, his crimson eyes gleaming with a mix of amusement and hunger. "You dare to awaken me, Count Vlad? Prepare for your doom!"

"Doom? Can we reschedule? I have homework due on Monday," Alex stammered, trying to inject some humor into the terrifying situation.

"Yeah, and I'm pretty sure my mom wouldn't appreciate a vampire in the living room," Mia added, her voice trembling.

The vampire let out a sinister laugh. "You have disturbed my slumber, and now you must pay the price. Your only hope is to complete the game. Fail, and you will join my legion of the undead."

More vampires began to materialize around them, each one more menacing than the last. The room was filled with cold, dark energy, and the air seemed to vibrate with an eerie hum.

"We have to keep playing," Mia whispered to Alex. "It's the only way to get rid of them."

They quickly moved to the next turn, each roll of the die bringing new challenges and more vampires. The house echoed with strange noises—whispers, growls, and the soft rustle of unseen wings.

Mia landed on a space that read, "Face the shadow beast. Defeat it, or be consumed by darkness." A card revealed a grotesque creature, all teeth and claws, waiting to be summoned.

Alex gulped. "I guess this beats math homework."

The shadow beast materialized, its eyes glowing malevolently. Mia grabbed a game piece shaped like a tiny, silver sword. "Alright, shadow beast. Bring it on."

The battle was tense, with the beast lashing out and Mia barely dodging its attacks. Alex cheered her on, making jokes to keep their spirits up.

"Come on, Mia! Pretend it's just a really big, ugly spider!"

With a final, well-aimed swipe, Mia defeated the shadow beast, and it vanished into thin air. They both breathed a sigh of relief.

"Nice job, Mia! Now it's my turn to fight something nasty, isn't it?" Alex said, rolling the die with determination.

As Alex landed on another perilous space, a hidden compartment in the game box popped open, revealing a tattered note. Mia quickly grabbed it and read aloud, "This game is a trap set by Count Vlad. The only way to reverse the curse and send the vampires back is to win the game."

Alex looked at her, his face pale. "So we're not just playing for fun. We're playing for our lives."

They steeled themselves, knowing that they had to outsmart Count Vlad and his minions. With every turn, they faced more challenges, but they also grew more determined. Their friendship and humor kept them going, even when things seemed darkest.

"We can handle this, Alex. We just have to stay one step ahead," Mia said, rolling the die and preparing for whatever the game would throw at them next.

The note they had found added a new layer of tension to the game. The realization that Count Vlad had set the game as a trap was terrifying, but it also gave Mia and Alex a new sense of purpose. They had to win, not just for themselves, but to protect their home from the vampire menace.

Mia looked at Alex, her eyes determined. "We've faced worse in gym class, right? We can handle this."

Alex nodded, though he couldn't help but crack a joke. "Yeah, like that time we had to dodgeball against the eighth graders. Piece of cake."

They continued to strategize, moving their pieces carefully, always trying to stay one step ahead of the vampires. Each turn brought new dangers, but also new opportunities to outsmart their foes.

The game threw increasingly difficult challenges at them. One space required them to solve a complex puzzle within a time limit, or face a swarm of bats. Another challenged them to a memory game, where failure meant being trapped in a maze of mirrors.

Mia and Alex tackled each challenge with a mix of determination and humor. When faced with the swarm of bats, Alex quipped, "I hope they don't poop on us. My mom just cleaned the carpets."

During the memory game, Mia joked, "At least this is better than studying for history class. Vampires are way more interesting than the Civil War."

Their banter kept them going, even when the challenges seemed insurmountable. With each victory, they grew more confident, their bond as friends strengthening.

Despite the fear and danger, Mia and Alex found moments to laugh and support each other. Their jokes and light-hearted comments not only eased the tension but also reminded them of why they were doing this together.

CHAPTER 3: THE BATTLE OF WITS

As the game progressed, the challenges became more intricate and difficult. One turn presented a riddle that seemed impossible to solve. Alex read aloud, "I speak without a mouth and hear without ears. I have no body, but I come alive with wind. What am I?"

Mia thought hard, pacing the room. "An echo!" she exclaimed finally. The game board reacted, moving their pieces forward.

"Nice one, Mia! We're getting the hang of this," Alex said, relieved.

Their next challenge involved navigating through a swarm of bats. The room darkened, and the sound of flapping wings filled the air. The bats swooped down, causing chaos and confusion.

Alex swatted at the air, trying to keep the bats at bay. "I hope they don't poop on us. My mom just cleaned the carpets!"

Mia laughed despite the tension. "Just keep moving, Alex! We have to get to the other side!"

They worked together, using pillows and blankets to fend off the bats, making their way to the next space on the board.

The following space transported them to a maze of mirrors. Reflections of themselves and the vampires seemed to stretch endlessly in all directions.

"This place is creeping me out," Alex said, his voice echoing.

"At least this is better than studying for history class. Vampires are way more interesting than the Civil War," Mia replied, trying to stay positive.

They navigated the maze by remembering the details of the real path versus the reflections. After a tense few minutes, they found their way out, much to their relief.

Despite the fear and danger, Mia and Alex found moments to laugh and support each other. Their jokes and light-hearted comments eased the tension and reminded them of why they were doing this together.

"If we solve this riddle, we get one step closer to winning," Mia said, reading a particularly tricky challenge.

"Or one step closer to becoming vampire snacks," Alex added with a grin.

"Don't worry, Alex. I'm pretty sure vampires don't like soccer players," Mia replied, rolling her eyes.

"Yeah, too much running involved," Alex shot back, making them both laugh.

As they navigated the board, their friendship became their greatest weapon. They knew that as long as they stuck together, they had a chance to win the game and send the vampires back where they belonged.

They moved their pieces strategically, planning their moves carefully to avoid the vampire spaces. With each roll of the die, they moved closer to the final showdown with Count Vlad, ready to face whatever the game would throw at them next.

Their determination and teamwork were unwavering. They had come too far to back down now. The final challenge was approaching, and they were prepared to face it head-on, with a mix of courage and humor.

CHAPTER 4: THE FINAL SHOWDOWN

The game had reached its climax. Mia and Alex could feel the tension in the air as they prepared for the final, high-stakes roll of the die. Count Vlad and his minions watched them with hungry eyes, eager to see them fail.

"Alright, Mia. This is it. The final roll," Alex said, handing her the blood-red die.

Mia took a deep breath, her hand shaking slightly. "Here goes nothing."

She rolled the die, and it landed on a space marked with a skull and crossbones. The board lit up, and a new challenge appeared: "Face Count Vlad in a final battle. Win, and you will be free. Lose, and you will join the undead."

Count Vlad stepped forward, his eyes gleaming with malevolent delight. "You have done well to come this far, but now you face the true master of the game. Prepare to be defeated!"

Mia and Alex exchanged a determined glance. They knew this was their last chance to win the game and send the vampires back. With a deep breath, they accepted the challenge.

The battle was fierce. Count Vlad was a formidable opponent, his powers far beyond anything they had faced before. But Mia and Alex fought with all their might, using every trick and strategy they had learned from the game.

Mia remembered a piece of advice from an earlier challenge and whispered to Alex, "Distract him while I figure out the pattern of his attacks."

Alex nodded and began taunting Count Vlad. "Hey, Count! Did anyone ever tell you that capes are so last century?"

Count Vlad snarled, "You insolent child!"

While the Count was distracted, Mia studied his movements, looking for a weakness. She noticed a slight hesitation in his attacks and realized that was her chance.

With a nod to Alex, Mia prepared to make her move. She timed it perfectly, striking during the Count's moment of hesitation. The vampire lord recoiled, hissing in pain.

"You may have found my weakness, but you will still fail!" Count Vlad roared.

Mia and Alex pressed on, exploiting the Count's weakness with precision. The battle reached its peak, and with a final, desperate move, Mia managed to outwit Count Vlad, completing the game and sending the vampires back into the board.

The room erupted in a blinding flash of light, and when it faded, the vampires were gone, and the game was over.

Mia and Alex collapsed onto the floor, exhausted but victorious.

"You may have won this time, but I will return!" Count Vlad's voice echoed faintly as he was pulled back into the game.

"Next time, bring some snacks. Preferably not us," Alex muttered, grinning weakly.

"Yeah, and maybe consider a hobby that doesn't involve cursing children," Mia added, her voice filled with relief.

They sat there for a moment, catching their breath and reveling in their victory. They had faced their fears, outsmarted the vampires, and won the game. Now, all that was left was to make sure no one ever unleashed the game's horrors again.

CHAPTER 5: THE AFTERMATH

Mia and Alex reflected on their adventure, realizing the importance of bravery, teamwork, and friendship. They had faced incredible danger and come out stronger for

it. The experience had taught them to believe in themselves and each other.

"We handled that pretty well, didn't we?" Mia said, her voice filled with awe.

"Yeah, and we didn't even need garlic bread," Alex replied with a chuckle.

They decided to store the game safely away, warning others about its dangers. They knew that the game was too powerful and too dangerous to be left where anyone could find it.

Just as they started to relax, they heard a faint whisper coming from the game box. Mia and Alex exchanged a nervous glance before carefully opening the box once more. Inside, they found a hidden compartment with a note from Mrs. Jenkins.

Mia read the note aloud, "Dear Mia and Alex, if you are reading this, then you have proven yourselves worthy. I am an ancient vampire hunter, and the game was a test to find my successors. The fight against the vampires is never-ending, and I need brave souls like you to continue my work."

Alex's eyes widened. "Mrs. Jenkins is a vampire hunter? Does this mean we get cool vampire-hunting gadgets?"

Mia laughed, "Only if they come with garlic bread."

The revelation was both shocking and exciting. Mia and Alex realized that their adventure was far from over. They had been chosen to carry on Mrs. Jenkins' legacy, to protect their town from the hidden threats that lurked in the shadows.

"Look, Alex, another weird artifact," Mia said, holding up a strange, ancient-looking amulet. "Should we buy it?"

"Only if it doesn't come with vampires or homework," Alex replied, grinning.

"Deal. Let's see what kind of trouble we can get into next!"

With their newfound purpose and a sense of excitement for the future, Mia and Alex prepared for their next adventure. They began researching vampire lore, learning everything they could about how to fight and defeat these ancient creatures.

They also started practicing their skills, turning their backyard into a training ground. They set up obstacles and challenges to keep themselves sharp and ready for whatever might come their way.

Their bond as friends grew even stronger as they trained and prepared for their new roles as vampire hunters. They knew that they would face many more dangers and challenges, but they were ready to face them together.

With a mix of courage, humor, and determination, Mia and Alex embarked on their new journey, ready to protect their town from the shadows that lurked just out of sight. The Vampire's Bloodthirsty Game was just the beginning of their incredible adventures, and they couldn't wait to see what came next.

The Blood Red Lake

CHAPTER 1: THE DISCOVERY

The family car rolled to a stop, sending a puff of dust into the air. Mark and Lisa, brimming with excitement, leaped out. Pine Hollow was a scene straight out of a nature documentary—massive trees reached up to the sky, and the forest was alive with the melodies of birds and the rustling of leaves.

Their parents were already unpacking. "Kids, help us set up the tent," Mom called out.

Reluctant to leave the car, Mark asked, "Lisa, do you think they have Wi-Fi here?"

Rolling her eyes, Lisa replied, "Mark, it's a campsite, not a hotel."

Mark sighed dramatically. "How will I survive without my cat videos?"

"We're here to enjoy nature, not the internet," Lisa said, grinning.

Mom interrupted their banter. "Kids, focus on the tent. Mark, stop pretending the tent poles are lightsabers."

Mark laughed, twirling a pole. "But I must defeat the evil Darth Tent!"

Their dad smiled. "Darth Tent, huh? Well, make sure he doesn't defeat us first."

Despite Mark's antics, the tent was set up quickly. Being seasoned campers, the family gathered firewood and organized their gear efficiently, soon having a cozy campsite ready.

The sky was a bright blue, dotted with fluffy clouds. Birds hopped from branch to branch, and the scent of pine filled the air. Mark and Lisa, buzzing with excitement, couldn't wait to explore.

"Ready for some fun?" Mark asked.

Lisa nodded eagerly. "Absolutely!"

The forest was a realm of untapped adventure. Mark and Lisa raced through the trees, their laughter ringing out. They stumbled upon a babbling brook, its water glistening under the sun, and waded in, playfully splashing each other.

Mark paused, his ears pricking up. "Did you hear that? Do you think it's Bigfoot?"

Lisa giggled. "Maybe it's just a squirrel. Or Bigfoot's pet squirrel!"

"Either way, I'm ready for an adventure!"

They ventured deeper into the woods, discovering odd mushrooms, curious insects, and trees with gnarled roots that seemed to tell ancient stories. The forest floor was a mosaic of fallen leaves, moss-covered stones, and delicate wildflowers. Each step unveiled new wonders.

As they continued, they found a fallen tree forming a natural bridge over a small ravine. Mark, ever the daredevil, climbed up first.

"Come on, Lisa! This is amazing!"

Lisa hesitated, eyeing the drop below. "Are you sure it's safe?"

"Totally! Just follow me."

With a deep breath, Lisa followed her brother. The bridge wobbled a bit, but they made it across safely, their hearts pounding with excitement.

Beyond the ravine, they discovered a grove of ancient trees with twisted, gnarled trunks. The branches formed a canopy, creating a cool, shaded retreat. They sat on a fallen log, catching their breath and soaking in the serene beauty.

"This place is incredible," Lisa said, wide-eyed.

"Yeah, it's like our own secret hideout," Mark agreed.

Their moment of peace was interrupted by a rustling in the bushes. Mark's eyes widened. "Did you hear that? Do you think it's Bigfoot?"

Lisa snickered. "Maybe it's just a squirrel. Or Bigfoot's pet squirrel!"

As they explored, they found a narrow, overgrown path. Mark, ever curious, pushed through the brush.

"Lisa, look at this trail! It looks like it leads to something cool."

"Or something creepy. Last one there is a rotten egg!"

"You're always a rotten egg, Mark."

"I prefer 'awesome explorer,' thank you very much."

The trail led them to a secluded lake, its water crystal clear, reflecting the vibrant greens of the forest. It felt like a hidden oasis.

They changed into their swimsuits and jumped in, the cool water a refreshing escape from the summer heat. The lake was deeper than it seemed, and they floated on their backs, gazing up at the sky through the leafy canopy.

"This place is amazing," Lisa said, her voice filled with awe.

"Yeah, it's like our own private paradise," Mark agreed.

They swam and splashed, enjoying the freedom and adventure. The water was refreshing, and the surrounding forest created a peaceful atmosphere.

After a while, they climbed out and lay on the grassy shore, letting the sun dry their skin. Mark's mind wandered back to the hidden trail that had led them here.

"Do you think anyone else knows about this place?" he wondered aloud.

Lisa shrugged. "Maybe, but it feels like it's been forgotten."

After their swim, they headed back to the campsite. They found an old man, Mr. Smith, talking with their parents.

"Kids, this is Mr. Smith. He's been coming to Pine Hollow for years," Dad said.

Mr. Smith nodded in greeting. "You kids shouldn't be poking around that lake. At sunset, it turns blood red."

"Blood red? Like ketchup? Is it a giant ketchup factory?" Mark asked, eyes wide.

"Mark, not everything is about food," Lisa groaned.

Mr. Smith chuckled. "Legend says a vampire lives at the bottom, cursed until he can find someone to break the curse."

"Cool! Wait, does he sparkle in the sun?"

"That's only in the movies, Mark," Lisa said, rolling her eyes.

Mr. Smith's expression turned serious. "It's just a story, but it's one that has kept people away from that lake for a long time. Best to leave it be."

Mark and Lisa exchanged a glance. They were intrigued, but they could see that their parents were not.

"Time to get ready for dinner," Mom said, breaking the tension. "We've got marshmallows for roasting."

As the family gathered around the campfire, the legend of the blood-red lake lingered in their thoughts. The fire crackled, casting dancing shadows, and the aroma of roasting marshmallows filled the air.

Mark leaned over to Lisa and whispered, "We have to see it for ourselves. Tomorrow at sunset?"

Lisa nodded, her eyes shining with excitement. "Definitely."

They made a pact to return to the lake, unaware of the dangers that awaited them. The legend was more than just a story, and their curiosity would lead them into a world they couldn't have imagined.

CHAPTER 2: THE RED SUNSET

The next day, Mark and Lisa couldn't stop thinking about the lake. Mr. Smith's story kept replaying in their minds, both scaring and exciting them.

"We have to see this! A ketchup lake at sunset!" Mark said.

"For the last time, it's not ketchup!" Lisa replied, though she was curious too.

Unaware of their children's plans, their parents let them explore again in the afternoon. As sunset approached, they set off toward the hidden trail, hearts pounding with anticipation.

The forest seemed different as they walked. The shadows grew longer, and the air felt cooler. Birds quieted down, replaced by the sound of their footsteps crunching on the forest floor.

"Do you think it's true?" Lisa asked, her voice barely above a whisper.

"Only one way to find out," Mark replied, trying to sound braver than he felt.

They reached the lake just as the sun began to dip. The clear water started to change, turning a deep, ominous red. It was like watching a potion transform.

"Whoa, it's actually turning red! This is so freaky," Mark whispered.

"It's like the lake is bleeding. I can't look away," Lisa added.

"Bet it still tastes like tomatoes," Mark joked, trying to ease the tension.

"I'm not tasting that! It looks too creepy!" Lisa replied, shivering despite the warmth of the evening.

The transformation was both mesmerizing and terrifying. The red deepened, becoming almost black as the last rays of sunlight vanished. The once serene lake now looked like something out of a nightmare.

The trees around the lake seemed to close in, their branches casting eerie shadows on the red water. A cold wind blew, sending chills down their spines.

"We should go back," Lisa said, her voice trembling.

"Not yet. We need to see if anything else happens," Mark insisted, though he was scared too.

As they stood there, Mark noticed a pale figure with dark eyes on the opposite shore. The figure raised a hand, beckoning them closer.

"Did you see that? Someone's by the shore!" Mark said.

"Let's go say hi. Maybe it's the vampire!" Lisa suggested, her curiosity getting the better of her fear.

"Or maybe it's just a guy who loves night fishing," Mark replied, though he didn't move.

"At a blood-red lake? Sounds fishy to me," Lisa retorted.

Before they could decide what to do, the figure vanished into the night, leaving them standing by the eerily transformed lake with more questions than answers.

The moon rose, casting a silvery light over the scene. The lake, now a dark, foreboding red, seemed to pulse with a life of its own. Mark and Lisa shivered, feeling a sense of foreboding.

"We should really go," Lisa said, pulling on Mark's arm.

"Yeah, you're right," Mark agreed, his bravado fading.

As they walked back to the campsite, the forest seemed darker, more menacing. Shadows stretched longer, and

the air grew colder. Strange whispers followed them through the trees, making them jump at every sound.

"Did you hear that whisper? It said 'leave,'" Mark said, his voice shaky.

"It's just the wind, Mark. Don't freak out," Lisa replied, moving closer to him.

"Wind or not, I'm sticking close to you," Mark admitted, not caring if it made him sound scared.

"That's a first," Lisa said with a small smile, though she was just as uneasy.

They quickened their pace, the sense of dread growing with each step. The path seemed longer than before, and every rustle of leaves made them jump. By the time they reached the campsite, they were breathless and jittery.

Their parents were sitting by the fire, oblivious to the children's ordeal. Mark and Lisa exchanged a glance, silently agreeing not to mention the lake for now. They joined their parents, the warmth of the fire a welcome contrast to the cold fear that had gripped them.

As they settled in for the night, the legend of the blood-red lake loomed larger in their minds. The experience had left them rattled, and they couldn't shake the feeling

that something dark and dangerous was lurking beneath the surface.

CHAPTER 3: THE VAMPIRE'S PLEA

That night, Mark had a vivid dream. He was back at the lake, but this time the water was calm and clear. A figure emerged from the depths—a vampire with piercing blue eyes and a regal bearing. The vampire introduced himself as Alistair.

"I need your help," Alistair said, his voice echoing in Mark's mind. "I was cursed centuries ago. Only you can break the curse."

Mark woke up in a cold sweat, his heart racing. The dream felt too real to be a mere figment of his imagination. He had to tell Lisa.

"Lisa, I had the weirdest dream. A vampire named Alistair needs our help," Mark said, shaking her awake.

Lisa groaned, rubbing her eyes. "Are you sure it wasn't from all those marshmallows you ate?"

"Positive. I think we should go back to the lake."

Lisa sighed. "Fine, but if it turns out you just want more marshmallows, I'm leaving you there."

At breakfast, Mark recounted his dream to Lisa. She listened intently, her skepticism fading as she saw how serious he was.

"Alright, let's do this. We need to help Alistair break the curse," Mark said, determination in his voice.

"I hope this isn't just an excuse for more night fishing," Lisa replied, though she was clearly intrigued.

"Or more ketchup," Mark added with a grin.

They packed a backpack with supplies—flashlights, snacks, and a notepad to take notes. As the sun began to set, they slipped away from the campsite, heading back to the hidden trail.

The forest seemed to hold its breath as they walked, the air heavy with anticipation. Mark and Lisa moved quickly, their determination overcoming their fear.

At the lake, they saw Alistair again, standing by the shore. This time, he spoke to them, explaining the curse that had trapped him for centuries.

"Thank you for returning. My curse is ancient and powerful, and I need your help to break it," Alistair said, his voice tinged with desperation.

"Do we get superpowers if we help you? Like, can I fly?" Mark asked, his excitement bubbling over.

"Or at least glow in the dark?" Lisa added.

Alistair smiled sadly. "I can promise you safety. I need you to perform a ritual to free me. Here is a list of items you need to gather: strange herbs, a silver dagger, and an ancient book of spells."

Mark and Lisa exchanged a glance. They were in deep now, but they couldn't back out. They agreed to help, though a nagging feeling warned them something wasn't quite right.

Mark and Lisa spent the next few days gathering the items. They found strange herbs in a clearing, their pungent aroma filling the air. The silver dagger was hidden in a hollow tree, glinting ominously in the sunlight. The ancient book of spells was the hardest to find. They located it in an abandoned cabin deep in the woods, its pages filled with cryptic symbols and eerie illustrations.

"This place feels eerie. I thought I saw something move," Mark whispered, clutching the book.

"You're just spooking yourself. Let's get out of here quickly," Lisa urged, her eyes scanning the dark corners.

They returned to the lake with the items, each carrying an eerie aura. The tension was palpable as they prepared for the ritual.

The sun was setting, casting long, chilling shadows across the forest. Mark and Lisa worked quickly, arranging the herbs in a circle, placing the silver dagger in the center, and opening the ancient book to the page Alistair had indicated.

Alistair appeared, looking both hopeful and desperate. "Thank you. The ritual must be performed exactly as the book says," he instructed.

Mark and Lisa nodded, their hearts pounding. They began the ritual, chanting the incantations and making the required gestures. The lake started to bubble and churn, a thick, red mist rising from its surface and enveloping them.

Chapter 4: The Ritual

Mark and Lisa spent days gathering the items. The herbs were in a remote clearing, the silver dagger in a hollow tree, and the ancient book in an abandoned cabin. Each find brought them closer to breaking the curse, but also increased their fear.

"We need to find herbs, a silver dagger, and an ancient book of spells," Mark said.

"Do we get a shopping cart for this treasure hunt?" Lisa joked.

"And can we stop for ice cream along the way?"

Their tasks were challenging. Thorny bushes scratched their arms, climbing the tree for the dagger was risky, and the cabin felt downright spooky.

"Do you ever feel like we're not alone here? I think I saw something in the shadows," Mark whispered, clutching the book.

"It's just your nerves. Let's hurry and get this done," Lisa urged, her eyes scanning the dark corners.

They returned to the lake, each item carrying an eerie aura. The tension was palpable as they prepared for the ritual.

On the night of the ritual, they prepared everything by the lake. The air was thick with tension, the sky dark with clouds. Alistair appeared, looking hopeful and desperate.

"Alright, we've got everything. Let's set it up," Mark said.

"Mark, that's not how you hold a dagger. You're not Zorro," Lisa corrected.

"En garde! I mean, uh, let's break this curse!"

They arranged the herbs in a circle, placed the dagger in the center, and opened the book to the marked page. Alistair guided them through each step. The lake, turning red once again with the setting sun, seemed to pulse with anticipation.

As they began, the air grew colder, the sky darker. They chanted and gestured, the lake bubbling and churning, a thick, red mist rising.

As they performed the ritual, the lake began to bubble. A thick mist rose, enveloping them. Alistair's appearance grew more sinister. They realized too late that breaking the curse would unleash a greater evil.

"Whoa, the lake is bubbling! Did we just make vampire soup?" Mark joked.

"I think we unleashed something much worse than soup," Lisa replied.

The mist thickened, Alistair's form shifting and twisting. His eyes glowed with malevolent light, his voice deepening.

"You have unleashed my power, and now I will restore my dominion," Alistair declared, his voice growing darker.

Mark and Lisa backed away, realizing their mistake. They had freed a dark sorcerer.

With the ritual complete, Alistair's true nature was revealed. His voice deepened, a dark power radiating from him. Mark and Lisa backed away in horror, their faces pale and their hearts pounding.

"You're not just a vampire, are you? What are you really?" Mark asked, his voice shaking.

"I had a feeling there was more to this. It's never simple, is it?" Lisa added, her eyes narrowing.

Alistair smirked, shadows swirling around him like a living shroud. "Fools! You have no idea what you've unleashed. My power is beyond your comprehension."

Mark and Lisa felt a deep sense of dread settle in. They had to stop him, but how? The items were meant to break the curse, not fight a sorcerer. They needed a plan.

"Go! We need to outrun him before he does something terrible!" Mark yelled, panic evident in his voice.

"Like making us scrub the entire house!" Lisa added, trying to keep things light despite the fear gripping her.

"Honestly, I'd take turning into a toad over that," Mark muttered under his breath.

They used the herbs to create a smokescreen, the dagger to cut through vines, and the book to cast faint glows of light, keeping the shadows at bay. But as they fled through the dense woods, Alistair's dark magic pursued them relentlessly.

The ground beneath them began to tremble as dark tendrils of magic snaked out from Alistair, wrapping around trees and rocks, drawing energy from the very earth. The lake, now clear and serene, started to bubble and churn once more, reflecting the chaos that Alistair was unleashing.

"Thank you for freeing me. Now I can reclaim my powers!" Alistair's voice resonated with newfound strength and menace.

Mark and Lisa stood frozen, realizing the magnitude of their mistake. "Wait, you were a dark sorcerer this whole time? Can we put you back?" Mark asked, his voice trembling.

Lisa's eyes widened in horror. "I knew there was a catch. There's always a catch."

Alistair's laughter echoed through the clearing, sending shivers down their spines. "Foolish children. You have no idea what you've unleashed. My power will now grow unchecked, and I will take over this world."

The air crackled with malevolent energy, and shadows seemed to reach out, trying to grab them.

CHAPTER 5: THE GREATER EVIL

Mark and Lisa exchanged a panicked glance. They had to get away from Alistair before it was too late. "Run! We need to get away from Alistair before he turns us into toads!" Mark shouted.

"Or worse, he makes us do more chores!" Lisa replied, trying to lighten the mood despite the fear gripping her heart.

"I'd rather be a toad than clean my room," Mark muttered, grabbing Lisa's hand as they sprinted towards the forest.

They fled through the dense woods, with Alistair's dark magic chasing them. The air crackled with malevolent energy, and shadows seemed to reach out, trying to grab them. They used the items they had gathered—strange herbs, the silver dagger, and the ancient book of spells—to create obstacles and slow him down. Mark threw the herbs into the air, creating a temporary barrier that held back the shadows.

Lisa quickly flipped through the book, searching for any spell that could help. "There has to be something in here!" she muttered, her fingers trembling.

They burst into a clearing near the campsite, realizing they had reached the place where it all began. The air was thick with tension, and the sky above was covered in dark clouds, creating an eerie atmosphere. The trees seemed to close in around them, their branches like skeletal arms reaching out to snare them.

"Quick, use the dagger and the book! We can trap him again!" Mark shouted, his voice filled with urgency.

Lisa nodded, her resolve strengthening. They began to chant the incantation from the ancient book, the runes glowing with a fierce light. The ground beneath them seemed to pulse with energy, the air vibrating with a malevolent force.

Alistair emerged from the shadows, his form twisted and menacing. His eyes glowed with a dark, unholy light, and shadows clung to him like a second skin. His body began to elongate and distort, with grotesque appendages emerging from his back, resembling the spindly legs of a monstrous spider.

"You dare defy me?" Alistair's voice boomed, shaking the very ground they stood on. The trees around them trembled, their leaves rustling like whispers of doom.

Mark and Lisa felt an icy chill run down their spines, but they held their ground. "Take that, evil sorcerer! And no, you don't get dessert!" Lisa shouted, her voice steady despite the fear coursing through her veins.

Alistair's laughter echoed through the clearing, a haunting and malevolent sound. "You think your childish incantations can stop me? I will crush you!" He raised his arms, and the shadows around him surged forward, transforming into grotesque, nightmarish creatures with gaping mouths and razor-sharp claws.

The creatures lunged at Mark and Lisa, their eyes glowing with a malevolent hunger. Mark swung the silver dagger, slicing through the nearest creature, which disintegrated into a cloud of dark mist with an ear-piercing screech. Lisa continued to chant, her voice growing stronger and more confident with each word.

The runes on the ground glowed brighter, casting an otherworldly light across the clearing. Alistair roared in fury, sending waves of dark energy towards them. The energy crackled through the air, distorting the very fabric of reality around them. The trees twisted and

writhed, their branches snapping and contorting into grotesque shapes.

"Keep chanting! We can't let him break our concentration!" Mark yelled, his voice barely audible over the cacophony of the battle.

Lisa's eyes were fixed on the ancient book, her voice unwavering. "By the power of the ancient runes, we bind you, Alistair! Back to the depths from which you came!"

Alistair's form began to flicker and distort, his power struggling against the binding spell. "No! I will not be defeated by mere children!" He summoned a vortex of shadows, which swirled around him like a dark cyclone, drawing in everything in its path.

The vortex pulled at Mark and Lisa, threatening to tear them from the ground. They clung to each other, their determination unshaken. "We have to finish this!" Mark shouted, his grip on the dagger tightening.

As the final words of the incantation left Lisa's lips, the runes erupted with blinding light. The vortex of shadows was torn apart, and Alistair's form began to disintegrate. His screams echoed through the forest, a sound of pure agony and rage. His grotesque appendages melted away, and his body was pulled back towards the lake.

The lake's water surged once more, turning a deep, ominous red. The thick, red mist rose from the water, enveloping Alistair. He screamed again, a sound that seemed to pierce the fabric of reality. His form continued to disintegrate, his dark power unraveling as he was pulled back into the depths of the lake.

"No! You cannot do this! I will return! I will always return!" Alistair's voice faded into a whisper as his form dissolved into the water.

The mist swirled around the clearing before dissipating, leaving the air clear and still. The ground stopped shaking, and the eerie glow from the runes faded. The forest fell silent, as if holding its breath.

Mark and Lisa collapsed to the ground, exhausted but victorious. They had done it—they had trapped Alistair once more. The grotesque creatures that had attacked them were gone, and the shadows had retreated, leaving the clearing bathed in the moon's soft light.

With the ritual complete, the forest fell silent. The air grew still, and the shadows retreated. Mark and Lisa stood by the now-calm lake, their hearts pounding. They had done it—they had trapped Alistair once more.

"Phew, we did it. Alistair is back in the lake," Mark said, his voice a mixture of relief and exhaustion.

Lisa nodded, her eyes filled with determination. "No more vampire lakes or dark sorcerers for us. Agreed?"

"Agreed. But next time, let's find a campsite with Wi-Fi," Mark replied, trying to lighten the mood.

"And no vampires," Lisa added with a chuckle.

"Or at least vampires that serve ketchup," Mark joked, earning a laugh from Lisa.

As they made their way back to the campsite, the forest seemed to watch them, its secrets hidden in the shadows. The trees no longer felt like ominous figures, but rather silent guardians of the secrets they held. The path seemed longer, and every rustle of leaves and snap of twigs made them jumpy, but they pressed on.

When they reached the campsite, their parents were packing up, unaware of the peril their children had faced. Mark and Lisa exchanged a knowing glance. They had faced a great evil and survived, but they knew their adventure was far from over.

The family left Pine Hollow, and Mark and Lisa carried the secret of the Blood Red Lake with them. They knew the danger was still there, but they also knew they had the courage to face it if it ever returned. The lake remained a haunting memory, a reminder of the thin line between curiosity and danger.

As they drove away, the shadows of the forest seemed to stretch out, watching them. But Mark and Lisa were no longer afraid. They had faced the darkness and emerged stronger. They had each other, and together, they knew they could face any challenge that came their way.

"Next time, let's choose a place with fewer supernatural threats," Lisa said, breaking the silence.

"Agreed. But if we do encounter another curse, at least we know what to do," Mark replied, a smile tugging at his lips.

"And we'll be ready," Lisa said firmly.

As the car drove further away from Pine Hollow, the forest closed in behind them, guarding its secrets. But for Mark and Lisa, the adventure had strengthened their bond and prepared them for whatever might come next.

And so, the story of the Blood Red Lake came to an end, but the bond between Mark and Lisa grew stronger. They were ready for whatever came next, knowing that together, they could face any challenge.

Camp Bloodwood

Chapter 1: The Legend Begins

Emma squinted through the smudged window of the old camp bus as it rumbled down the bumpy, tree-lined road. Camp Bloodwood, with its towering pines and dense underbrush, seemed like the perfect setting for an adventure. Beside her, Nate was fiddling with his beat-up baseball cap, making faces at Maya, who was deeply engrossed in her book. The excitement in the air was palpable, mingled with the scent of pine and the distant calls of forest birds.

The bus came to a creaky stop, and the kids poured out, dragging their suitcases and backpacks. Emma looked around, taking in the sprawling campgrounds. There were wooden cabins arranged in a semicircle, a large mess hall, and a rickety old dock jutting out into a sparkling lake. It looked exactly like she had imagined — maybe even better.

"Welcome to Camp Bloodwood!" boomed a cheerful voice. Emma turned to see a tall, lanky man with a toothy grin and a camp counselor's uniform. "I'm Mike, your head counselor. We're going to have an amazing summer!"

Emma smiled, feeling a surge of excitement. She glanced at Nate, who was already pretending to joust with his

suitcase, and Maya, who had tucked her book under her arm and was looking around curiously.

They spent the next hour unpacking and settling into their cabin. The wooden bunks creaked with every move, and the small windows let in just enough light to keep the place from feeling too claustrophobic. Emma took the top bunk, Nate the bottom, and Maya chose the bed nearest the window.

As evening fell, the counselors gathered all the campers around a large campfire. The flames danced and flickered, casting eerie shadows on the kids' faces. Mike stood up, his face illuminated by the firelight, and raised his hands for silence.

"Now, who here likes ghost stories?" he asked with a mischievous grin. Hands shot up all around the circle, including Emma's. "Great! Because Camp Bloodwood has a very special one."

He leaned in closer, his voice dropping to a whisper. "Legend has it that a vampire roams these woods. It only comes out at night, searching for campers who wander too far from their cabins..."

The fire crackled, and the campers leaned in, wide-eyed. Emma felt a chill run down her spine, but she couldn't help but feel intrigued. Nate snickered beside her, clearly

not taking the story seriously, while Maya hugged her knees, her eyes darting nervously around.

After the story, the kids were sent to their cabins. As they walked back, Nate was still chuckling. "A vampire in the woods? They really want to scare us, don't they?"

Emma shrugged. "Who knows? Maybe there's some truth to it."

Maya shivered. "I hope not. I don't want to meet any vampires."

Later that night, as the sounds of the forest began to settle into a rhythmic lull, Emma lay awake in her bunk, staring at the ceiling. She couldn't shake the story from her mind. She glanced over at Nate, who was still grinning to himself in the dim light of their cabin.

"Nate," she whispered, "what if we went to look for this vampire?"

Nate's eyes lit up with mischief. "Now you're talking! What do you say, Maya?"

Maya looked horrified at the suggestion. "Are you serious? What if there really is something out there?"

Emma climbed down from her bunk and sat next to Maya. "Come on, Maya. It'll be fun. We'll just take a quick look around and come right back."

Nate grabbed his flashlight. "Exactly. We'll be like detectives. Detective Nate and his brave team!"

Maya sighed, closing her book reluctantly. "Fine. But if we get caught, I'm blaming you two."

Sneaking out of the cabin was easier than they expected. The night air was cool and crisp, and the forest seemed even more mysterious under the cover of darkness. Their flashlights cast long beams of light, illuminating the path ahead.

They ventured deeper into the woods, with Nate leading the way, Emma right behind him, and Maya sticking close to Emma's side. The sounds of crickets and distant hoots of owls filled the air, creating a symphony of nighttime noises.

Suddenly, Nate stopped, pointing his flashlight at a set of footprints. "Look at these! They're huge."

Emma leaned in to examine them. "They don't look like any animal prints I've seen."

Maya looked around nervously. "Can we go back now? This place gives me the creeps."

Just then, they heard a rustling noise from the bushes. They froze, their hearts pounding. The flashlight flickered, and Emma tightened her grip on it.

"Who's there?" Nate called out bravely, though his voice wavered slightly.

A pair of glowing eyes stared back at them from the darkness. The creature moved swiftly, and the kids' flashlights flickered wildly, casting erratic shadows.

"Run!" Emma shouted, grabbing Maya's hand. They bolted back to their cabin, their footsteps pounding against the forest floor. The eerie noises of the forest seemed to chase after them.

Back in the safety of their cabin, they collapsed onto their bunks, panting and wide-eyed. "What was that?" Maya whispered, her voice trembling.

"I don't know," Emma admitted. "But whatever it was, it's real."

CHAPTER 2: STRANGE HAPPENINGS

The next morning, the trio woke up feeling a mix of excitement and apprehension. They couldn't stop thinking about the previous night's encounter. As they headed to the mess hall for breakfast, Nate was still buzzing with curiosity.

"We need to figure out what those footprints were," he said between bites of scrambled eggs. "And who or what those eyes belonged to."

Emma nodded, her mind racing. "Let's check around our cabin first. Maybe there's more evidence."

After breakfast, they made their way back to their cabin and started searching the area. Nate, ever the jokester, pretended to be a detective, examining every leaf and twig with exaggerated seriousness.

"Detective Nate on the case!" he declared, making Emma and Maya giggle.

Their laughter was cut short when they found a set of unusual footprints leading behind their cabin. The prints were large and oddly shaped, unlike anything they had seen before.

"These are definitely not from any animal I've read about," Maya said, her voice tinged with worry.

As they followed the prints, they stumbled upon an old, crumbling gravestone hidden behind a thick bush. The name on the gravestone was scratched out, leaving it illegible.

"This is getting creepier by the minute," Emma said, her eyes wide with curiosity and fear.

Before they could investigate further, they heard the counselors approaching. Quickly, they hid behind the cabin, peeking out to see what was happening.

The counselors were speaking in hushed tones, their expressions serious. "We need to keep an eye on the kids," Mike said. "They can't find out what's really going on."

Emma, Nate, and Maya exchanged worried glances. What could the counselors be hiding?

That night, as the camp settled into quiet, the trio made their plans. Emma, Nate, and Maya decided to sneak out once again, determined to uncover the secrets of Camp Bloodwood. This time, they were more cautious, moving silently through the woods.

The forest was even darker than before, and every rustle of leaves made them jump. They reached the area where they had seen the glowing eyes the previous night. The air was thick with tension.

Suddenly, they heard whispers around them, seemingly coming from nowhere. The whispers grew louder, and the kids could barely make out the words. "Leave now... before it's too late..."

Emma's flashlight flickered again, and they saw the same pale figure darting between the trees. The whispers seemed to follow them, growing more insistent.

"Let's get out of here!" Maya whispered urgently.

They sprinted back to their cabin, hearts pounding. Once inside, they bolted the door and huddled together, trying to make sense of what they had experienced.

"We need to find out more about this place," Emma said determinedly. "The counselors are definitely hiding something."

Nate nodded. "And I think it's time we find out what."

Chapter 3: Unveiling Secrets

The next day, they kept a close eye on the counselors, looking for any opportunity to investigate. During free time, they noticed Mike slipping away towards the main cabin. Seizing the moment, they followed him discreetly.

Mike entered a small, inconspicuous door at the back of the main cabin. Once he was out of sight, the trio approached the door. Emma tried the handle, and to their surprise, it was unlocked.

Inside, they found a narrow staircase leading down to a hidden room. The room was dimly lit by flickering

candles, casting eerie shadows on the walls. Old books and strange artifacts were scattered around, creating an unsettling atmosphere.

Emma picked up a dusty old diary from a table. "Look at this," she whispered, flipping through the pages.

The diary detailed the history of Camp Bloodwood and its dark secrets. It revealed that in the early 1900s, Camp Bloodwood was a small settlement known as Bloodwood Village. The villagers were simple folk, relying on the dense forest and clear lake for their livelihood. However, the village was plagued by mysterious disappearances and strange occurrences, especially during the full moon.

Legend had it that a vampire, seeking refuge from hunters, found solace in the secluded village. The vampire, known as Count Mortis, began preying on the villagers. To protect themselves, the villagers built a church with a large cross that they believed would ward off the vampire. Despite their efforts, the vampire continued to terrorize the village.

Desperate, the villagers sought the help of a mysterious traveler who claimed to be a vampire hunter. Armed with ancient knowledge and powerful relics, this hunter managed to trap Count Mortis in a hidden underground chamber, sealing him away with powerful wards.

Years passed, and the village was abandoned. In the 1950s, the land was bought by a wealthy entrepreneur who saw the potential for a summer camp. He built cabins, a mess hall, and recreational facilities, transforming the eerie village into Camp Bloodwood. However, the history of the place was not forgotten, and the legends of the vampire persisted.

The camp counselors, descendants of the original villagers, knew of the hidden chamber and the vampire trapped within. They took it upon themselves to ensure that the vampire remained sealed, using the campfire stories to keep the legend alive and the campers wary of wandering too far into the woods.

As Emma read aloud, the room seemed to grow colder. Maya shivered, and Nate's usual bravado faded. "We need to get out of here," he said, his voice trembling.

Before they could leave, they heard footsteps approaching. They quickly hid behind a large bookshelf, holding their breath as the door creaked open. Mike entered the room, his expression stern and wary.

Mike scanned the room, his eyes narrowing as if sensing something was amiss. Emma, Nate, and Maya stayed perfectly still, hoping he wouldn't discover them.

After what felt like an eternity, Mike left, locking the door behind him. The trio let out a collective sigh of relief.

"We have to expose them," Emma whispered. "But how?"

Nate's eyes lit up with a mischievous glint. "I have an idea."

That night, they gathered all the campers around the campfire once again. This time, Emma, Nate, and Maya took center stage. Nate pulled out his portable speaker, and Emma gave a knowing nod.

CHAPTER 4: THE TRUTH REVEALED

As the campers settled, Emma began to speak. "We've discovered something about Camp Bloodwood that you all need to know."

Nate started the beat on his speaker, and the counselors, standing on the outskirts of the circle, looked confused. The campers watched, curious and intrigued.

Emma continued, "The counselors here are vampires. The stories, the legends — they're all true."

Gasps and murmurs spread through the crowd. The counselors stepped forward, their faces darkening with anger.

Nate stepped up, taking the lead with his playful yet defiant rap.

"Yo, counselors of the night, think you're outta sight, But you're lookin' kinda pale, like you lost a fight! We've got stakes and garlic, yeah, we came prepared, Gonna send you back to crypts, 'cause you're way too scared!"

The head counselor, clearly unamused, responded with a deep, ominous voice.

"You think you're tough, kids, but you're just outta luck, We've been around for centuries, while you still play with trucks! We control the night, with a single bite, We'll put you all to bed, and turn out the light!"

Emma jumped in, her voice steady and strong.

"You think you're so cool, with your dark vampire rule, But we've got courage and brains, and we won't be your fools! Your fangs don't scare us, and your capes are a joke, When we're done with you, you'll vanish in a puff of smoke!"

A second counselor, baring his fangs, joined the rap battle.

"You meddling kids, always causing a scene, But you're no match for us, we're the blood-sucking team! You

think you're so smart, with your little flashlights, We'll drain you of your fun and haunt your nights!"

Maya, usually quiet and reserved, stepped forward with a confident grin.

"We've read all the stories, we know how this goes, Sunlight and laughter, that's how the legend shows! So take your creepy tales and your nocturnal fright, 'Cause we're the kids of Bloodwood, and we own the night!"

The counselors, now visibly frustrated, spoke in unison, their voices blending into a haunting chorus.

"You kids are brave, we'll give you that, But against our fangs, you'll fall flat! This is our camp, our domain, our place, Now prepare yourselves to vanish without a trace!"

Nate finished with a flourish, his voice echoing through the trees.

"We're not scared, and we won't back down, We'll take you on, and reclaim our crown! With our friends by our side, we'll always fight, Goodbye, dear vampires, it's the end of your night!"

Chapter 5: A New Beginning

With the final verse, a beam of sunlight broke through the clouds, striking the vampires. They recoiled, hissing and retreating into the shadows. The campers cheered; their fear replaced with triumph.

The camp returned to normal, and Emma, Nate, and Maya were hailed as heroes. The trio basked in the admiration, exchanging funny and exaggerated stories about their adventure.

"Remember when Mike tried to rhyme 'trucks' with 'luck'?" Nate laughed. "He sounded like a rusty robot!"

Emma grinned. "And when Maya dropped that sunlight line? Classic!"

Maya blushed but smiled proudly. "Well, someone had to shut them up."

As the summer came to an end, Emma, Nate, and Maya packed up their things, ready to leave Camp Bloodwood. They felt a mixture of sadness and pride, knowing they had uncovered the camp's dark secrets and protected their fellow campers.

As they drove away, Emma glanced back and spotted a new counselor with a suspiciously familiar pale

complexion watching them. She shivered but then smiled, knowing that they were ready for anything that might come their way.

"You think there's another adventure waiting for us back home?" Nate asked, leaning back in his seat.

"Definitely," Emma replied. "And we'll be ready."

"Just no more vampires, please," Maya added, making them all laugh.

Hey there, fearless reader!

Did this book give you a good mix of laughs, gasps, and spooky chills?

If you had a blast with these stories, I've got a fun mission for you!

Imagine this book sitting on Amazon, lonely and shivering, waiting for your review to warm it up. Your thoughts can help other brave souls discover these adventures.

So, grab your flashlight, shake off those goosebumps, and leave a review on Amazon.

Thanks for being an amazing reader.

Let's keep the spooky fun going!

SCAN ME

Printed in Great Britain
by Amazon